The Little Mermaid
and Other Stories

Look for all the
SCHOLASTIC JUNIOR CLASSICS

SCHOLASTIC JUNIOR CLASSICS

The Little Mermaid
and Other Stories

Retold from
Hans Christian Andersen

by Sarah Hines Stephens

SCHOLASTIC INC.

New York   Toronto   London   Auckland   Sydney
Mexico City   New Delhi   Hong Kong   Buenos Aires

All rights reserved. Published by Scholastic Inc. SCHOLASTIC
and associated logos are trademarks and/or registered
trademarks of Scholastic Inc.

ISBN 0-439-29145-3

12 11 10 9 8 7   4 5 6/0

Printed in the U.S.A.   40

First Scholastic printing, March 2002

Contents

The
Little Mermaid
and Other Stories

The Little Mermaid

Chapter One

FAR from land, in the middle of the ocean, was a place where the water was crystal clear and blue as a forget-me-not. There, down very deep, was the place where the merpeople lived.

The merking's castle stood in the very deepest spot. The palace walls were made of coral. The roof was oyster shells. And the windows stood open to let the fish swim in and out.

A widower, the merking lived in his castle with his mother, the old queen. She was a proud woman who took great care of her six granddaughters.

The little princesses were lovely mermaids. The youngest was the most beautiful of all. She had skin like a rose petal, eyes as blue as the sea, and a colorful fish tail. Every morning the sisters would play in the castle halls, feeding fish and darting about in the water. Every afternoon they would tend their gardens.

You might think that the bottom of the ocean is covered in white sand like a beach. But in fact, many plants and flowers grew in the castle's large garden. Bright red and dark blue trees swayed, heavy with glittering fruit. Under these trees each princess had her own spot where she could dig and plant as she pleased.

One sister shaped her small garden like a whale. Another sister planted hers in the form of a mermaid. But the littlest mermaid made hers round and planted it full with red flowers so that it looked like the red ball of the sun when it shone deep down into the ocean.

Most of the princesses filled their gardens with strange objects they collected from wrecked ships. The youngest chose just one. In the middle of her rosy garden the little mermaid placed a marble statue of a boy. She loved to stare at the statue and listen to her grandmother tell tales of the world above.

Their grandmother told the sisters about ships and towns, people and animals. The mermaids listened to stories about fish that sang on tree branches (they were really birds), flowers with fragrance (flowers do not smell under the ocean), and other fantastic things.

The little mermaid longed to see these things for herself.

"When you are fifteen years old, you will be allowed to rise up to the surface of the sea," her grandmother said. "There you can sit on the rocks in the moonlight and watch the ships. If you are brave, you can swim close enough to see the forests and towns."

The eldest sister was nearly fifteen already, but the youngest would have to wait a full five years before she could go. The little mermaid could not wait. She did not complain, but at night she would stay by an open window in the castle, gazing up through the water at the moon and stars.

Chapter Two

WHEN the eldest sister returned from the surface of the sea, she had hundreds of stories to tell. The best thing, she said, was lying in the moonlight on a sandbank off the coast of a big town. From there she could watch the lights on land, twinkling like stars. She could hear the music and the hustle and bustle of the people. She could see the church spires and hear the ringing bells.

The little mermaid listened to every word. Later in the evening, when she gazed up through the open window, she imagined she could see church towers and hear the bustle and noise of a town.

When the second sister swam away the

following year, she rose out of the water just as the sun was setting. She claimed that this sight had to be the most beautiful. So glorious was the golden light and the purple and crimson of the clouds, she could barely describe it.

The third sister was the most daring. She swam up a wide river between beautiful green hills. She saw houses and castles tucked into magnificent woods. She heard birds sing (it was then she learned they were not fish) and even came across a group of children wading. The third sister would always remember the children who could swim even though they didn't have fish tails.

The fourth sister was timid. She stayed out in the middle of the sea but said it was the most beautiful of all. The sky stretched like a glass dome over her head, while all around her playful dolphins turned somersaults and big whales spouted like fountains.

The fifth sister's birthday came next. Since her birthday came in winter, she saw things the other sisters had not. When she broke the surface, the ocean was green and filled with floating icebergs. The icebergs were strangely shaped and glittered like diamonds. She sat on the largest one with her hair flowing around her, scaring passing sailors.

At first, each of the sisters was charmed by what she found above the surface of the sea. But eventually they grew tired of the world above, and all agreed that things were best below the waves, where they felt at home.

Still they did not stop going to the surface. When a storm was brewing, the sisters would rise arm in arm and sing to the sailors in their beautiful voices. They sang about their lovely world at the bottom of the sea and told the sailors not to be afraid of coming down.

Not yet fifteen, the littlest mermaid

would watch her sisters rise to the surface without her. Her longing to see the world above was so great she felt as if she would cry. But mermaids don't have tears, which makes them suffer all the more.

Chapter Three

AT last the little mermaid turned fifteen. The old queen placed a wreath of flowers in her hair and watched the youngest princess rise as lightly as a bubble through the water.

The little mermaid broke the surface of the water as the sun was setting. Nearby, a masted ship bobbed on the water. There was not a puff of wind, and the sailors sat on the ship's decks, singing and making music. As it grew dark, colored lamps were lit and hung in the rigging. A celebration was about to begin.

The little mermaid swam closer. When the waves lifted her, she could see into the cabin windows. There were many people dressed in rich clothing. The handsomest of all was a young prince. He had large dark eyes and looked to be about sixteen years old. In fact, he had just turned sixteen. The celebration was for his birthday!

The music grew louder, and sailors danced on the deck. When the prince came out, rockets were sent high into the night sky, lighting it up as bright as day. The little mermaid was frightened and ducked underwater. When she lifted her head again, it looked like the stars in the heavens were falling into the ocean. It was the first time she had seen fireworks.

Even with all of the things to see, the little mermaid could not keep her eyes off the prince. He was beautiful! She bobbed in the water, watching him smile and dance.

It was late, but still the little mermaid could not turn away. The music stopped and the lanterns were put out. The ship began to sail away, faster and faster as the sails were raised.

The waves grew. Black clouds bloomed on the horizon. A storm was brewing. As quickly as the sails went up, they came back down again. The waves around the ship were as big as mountains.

Suddenly, a wave broke over the ship and snapped its mast like a reed. The little mermaid watched as the ship was torn apart. She looked and looked for the young prince. At last, as the ship sank, she saw him.

Now he will come play under the waves with me, she thought joyfully. Then she remembered that humans cannot live underwater, and the prince would be dead before he ever reached her father's castle.

He must not die, she told herself. The little mermaid dived into the splintered wreckage. When she reached the prince, he was too tired to swim. His arms and legs were limp. He would have drowned if the little mermaid had not held his head above the water.

In the morning the storm was over. The sun rose, glowing red, and shone on the snowy peaks of blue mountains in the distance. At the base of the mountains was a green forest. And on the edge of the forest stood a white church with lemon and orange trees in front.

The little mermaid swam with her prince into the bay and laid him on the beach in front of the church. She carefully placed his head in the sunshine, admiring the color of his cheeks.

Church bells rang high up in the steeple, and a group of young girls came out to walk. The little mermaid swam behind some rocks, covered her head with seaweed, and watched to see what would happen to her poor prince.

It was not long before one of the girls discovered him. She called to the others.

When the prince awoke, he smiled up at them. The little mermaid was sad that the prince did not smile at her. But he did not know she was hiding in the bay. And he did not know it was she who had saved him. After the girls carried the prince away, the little mermaid felt more alone than she had in her whole life and dived down deep into the dark under the waves.

Chapter Four

THE youngest princess had always been quiet and thoughtful. Now she grew even more silent. Whenever she could, she returned to the place where she had last seen the prince. She saw the snow melt from the mountain peaks and watched the fruit ripen, but she never saw the prince.

When the little mermaid returned home to her underwater palace, she would kiss the statue in her garden, for it reminded her of the prince. But she did not tend her flowers. They grew and grew until they covered the paths and snaked into the trees, making the whole garden dark.

When she could bear her sorrow no longer, the little princess told one of her sisters about the prince. Soon they all knew and they shared the sad story with their closest friends. One of these friends knew who the prince was and where to find his kingdom.

The princesses wasted no time in telling the littlest mermaid. "Come, little sister," they said. They swam with her to the shore where the prince's castle stood. The castle was beautiful, with golden domes reaching up to the sky and marble stairs leading down to the sea.

Once the little princess knew where the prince lived, she spent many evenings there, swimming closer to the shore than any of her sisters had ever dared. She heard fishermen talking about how kind and good the prince was, and she was glad that she had saved him. At night she saw her prince standing alone on a marble balcony in the moonlight.

More and more the mermaid grew to love human beings. She wished she could leave the sea to live among them. Their world seemed so much bigger than hers. She wanted to walk through the fields that seemed to stretch forever, ride in carriages through forests, and climb the mountains that stood high above the clouds.

She had so many questions about the land above.

"If a human does not drown, will he live forever?" the little mermaid asked her grandmother. "Or do they die as the river merpeople do?"

"Yes, they also die," the old queen said. "And their life is shorter than ours. But when we die, we are turned to foam on the water. Human beings have souls that live forever and ever. When they die, humans rise through the air to the shinning stars to dwell forever and see things we shall never see."

"I would trade anything to live one day as a human and the rest of eternity in the heavens," the little mermaid sighed. "Is there nothing I can do to get a soul and live with the humans?" the princess asked.

"Only if a human should fall so in love with you that you were more important to him than anyone else and you were married. But that will never happen. Humans have no sense. They think our lovely fish tails are ugly and that you must have two legs to be beautiful."

The little mermaid sighed and looked down at her fish tail.

"Think no more about it," her grandmother said. "Let us be happy we can swim and jump through the waves for three hundred years. That is time enough. And remember, tonight your father is holding a court ball."

Chapter Five

THE splendor of the court ball was something that could only be seen in the depths of the ocean. Hundreds of green and pink oyster shells lined the great glass hall. Colorful fish, big and small, swam close to the glass walls. A great current swept through the hall, and the mermen and mermaids danced upon it.

The merpeople have voices more beautiful than any heard on land, and they took turns singing to one another at the ball. The little mermaid's voice was loveliest of all, and everyone clapped when she was finished. For a moment she felt happy.

But she could not forget the handsome prince. She swam quietly away to her small garden where she gazed up toward the surface of the water.

I love him more than anything, she thought. More than my father and my grandmother. I would do anything to win him and an immortal soul. Anything so that I might be with him forever.

At that moment the little mermaid knew what she must do. Although the thought frightened her, she would go to the seawitch and ask for her help.

The little mermaid swam far from the castle, beyond a violent whirlpool, past the bubbling mud bog, to the place where the seawitch lived.

The seawitch's house sat in a strange forest. It was surrounded by bushes that were half plant and half animal. They looked like wriggling snakes with hundreds of heads and slimy, wormlike fingers. If those fingers caught something, they would never let go.

Filled with dread, the little mermaid

stood at the entrance to the forest. Her heart pounded in fear. She almost turned back. But when she thought of the prince, her courage returned.

The little mermaid braided her hair and wound it tightly around her head. Holding her arms close to her body, she swam quickly through the water. The ugly plants stretched out their fingers and tried to grab her.

At last the plants thinned, and the little mermaid found herself in a slimy place where fat eels played in the mud. In the center, made from the bones of drowned sailors, was the seawitch's house. And in the doorway sat the seawitch, feeding a toad and petting the eels in her lap.

"I know what you want," she cackled when she saw the little mermaid. "You want to trade your lovely fish tail for a pair of ugly stumps so the prince will fall in love with you." The witch laughed so evilly that the toad and eels jumped down into the mud.

The little mermaid could say nothing.

"It is stupid of you," she said. "But you shall have your wish, little princess, though it will bring you misery. I will mix you a potion. Tomorrow you will drink it sitting on a beach. Your tail will divide and shrink into human legs. It will hurt — like a sword running through you — and although you will walk with the grace of a dancer, every step you take on land will feel as if you are walking on knives. If you are willing to suffer this, I can help you."

"I am," the princess whispered, for she would suffer anything for the prince.

"Once you have a human body you can never be a mermaid again," the witch screeched. "Never again will you swim with your sisters or see your father's castle. If you fail to make the prince love you so that he thinks of nothing else and begs you to marry him, the morning after he marries another you will become foam on the ocean."

The little mermaid was pale. "I must try," she whispered.

"You will have to pay me, too," the witch grinned, "with the most precious thing you have — your beautiful voice."

"But if you take my voice —" The mermaid gasped.

"I suppose you thought you could use it to charm your prince," the witch hissed through thin lips. "But you will still have a graceful walk and your lovely eyes. Speak with them."

The witch dripped her own blood into a cauldron, along with the other ingredients. When it reached a rolling boil, the steam from the pot rose in the shapes of strange creatures. When at last it was finished, it looked like clear water.

"Here it is," said the witch. She quickly

cut out the little mermaid's tongue so she could neither speak nor sing.

The little mermaid hurried from the witch's house. The terrible plants cowered when they saw the potion the princess held in her hands.

When she arrived at the palace, it was dark. The ball was over and everyone was asleep. The little mermaid could not go to her sisters. Even if she could speak, she could not bring herself to tell them that she was going away forever. Instead she picked a flower from each of their gardens and threw a hundred finger kisses toward the palace. Then she swam up through the deep blue sea.

Chapter Six

WHEN the sun peeked over the horizon, it found the little mermaid sitting on the marble steps of the prince's castle. There she drank the potion. The pain in her tail was so great that she fainted.

When she awoke, she could still feel a burning pain — but standing in front of her, gazing upon her with his dark eyes, was the prince. The little mermaid looked down and saw that her fish tail was gone. In its place were two lovely legs.

"Who are you and how did you get here?" the prince asked. The mermaid could only look at him sadly. When she did not answer, the prince took her hand and led her gently up to his castle.

In the castle the little mermaid was dressed in royal clothes. At dinner she sat beside the prince. Oh, how she longed to speak and to tell the prince she had saved him!

When the palace singers came out to perform, one young girl sang better than all the rest. The prince clapped his hands and smiled at the singer.

If only he knew I have given away my lovely voice to be with him, the little mermaid thought.

The palace dancers came next, and the little mermaid rose onto her toes to dance with them. She floated across the floor. No one had ever seen anyone dance as beautifully as she did. Her sad eyes and flowing movements told much more than the singers' song had.

Everyone was delighted, especially the

prince. The little mermaid danced again and again, even though the pain she felt each time her foot touched the floor was terrible.

The prince was enchanted and declared that she could never leave him. That night and every night after she slept on a velvet pillow in front of the prince's door. Each day she accompanied him on rides through green forests. She heard birds sing and ran through fields. She climbed mountains so high her feet bled. But she paid them no mind and climbed higher, following her prince, until they could look down and see the clouds.

Some nights when everyone was asleep, the little mermaid would walk down the marble stairs and cool her feet in the ocean.

One night her sisters came, arm in arm, singing sadly. They sang to her about how much they missed her. And once, far out at sea, the little mermaid saw her grandmother. It had been years since she had put her head above the waves. And there beside the queen was the little mermaid's father, in his crown. Together they stretched their hands toward the youngest princess but did not dare come close to shore.

Chapter Seven

DAY by day the prince grew to love the little mermaid, but he loved her as he would a child.

"Don't you love me more than all others?" the mermaid asked with her eyes.

"You are dear to me," the prince told her, "and you have the kindest heart. You remind me of a girl who I will never see again. I was in a shipwreck and the waves carried me ashore. A young girl from a church found me on the beach and saved my life. I saw her only twice, but she is the only girl I can ever truly love."

The little mermaid sighed deeply, for she could not cry.

Time passed, and everyone said the prince was to be married to the neighboring king's daughter. A magnificent ship was made ready, and it was announced that the prince would be traveling to see the neighboring kingdom.

"When he comes back, he will bring his new wife," the people said.

The little mermaid shook her head and smiled. She knew what was in the prince's heart.

"I must go and meet this princess," the prince told her. "My parents demand it. But they cannot force me to marry her.

"If I do ever marry, I will probably marry you." The prince kissed the little mermaid and rested his head near her heart. And the little mermaid felt closer to human happiness than ever before.

Aboard the ship on the way to the neighboring kingdom, while everyone slept, the little mermaid sat and looked down into the clear water. Her sisters came and looked at her sadly, wringing their hands.

The next morning the ship sailed into the harbor of the neighboring kingdom. Church bells rang, trumpets blew, and banners waved. There were banquets and balls and parties. But the princess of the kingdom was not at any of them. She did not live in the palace. She lived in a church where she was learning all of the royal virtues.

The little mermaid longed to see the princess. When at last the princess appeared, the little mermaid had to admit that the princess was the most beautiful girl she had ever seen.

"It is you!" exclaimed the prince when he finally met the princess. "You are the one who saved me when I lay half dead on the beach!" The prince rushed to embrace his new bride-to-be.

"That which I dared not hope has happened," the prince told the little mermaid. "I know you will share my happiness, for I know you love me more than all others."

The little mermaid kissed the prince's hand. She felt as if her heart were breaking. The prince's wedding morning would bring her death, and she would become nothing but foam on the ocean.

Soon after the meeting between the prince and his princess, church bells rang. The little mermaid dressed in gold and silks and carried the train of the bride's dress, but she did not see the splendor of the ceremony or hear the music. Soon she would lose her prince and her life.

The bride and groom went aboard the prince's ship for the celebration. The sails were unfurled, and the ship glided across the crystal sea.

When evening came, colored lamps were lit and the sailors danced. The little mermaid could not help but remember when she had first lifted her head from the sea and seen the same sight.

With a pain in her heart far greater than the pain in her feet, the little mermaid danced like she had never danced before. She knew this was the last night she would see the prince, the man for whom she had given her voice and left her home and family. And he would never know her sacrifice.

The evening was filled with fun and splendor. The little mermaid laughed and smiled, though she had death in her heart. When the prince and princess finally went into their tent to sleep, the ship grew quiet.

The little mermaid stood, looking east. She was watching for the first pink of dawn. She knew that with the first sunbeam her life would end. Before the first light came, her sisters emerged from the sea. All of their hair had been cut off, and they held a knife out toward her.

"We've traded our hair to the seawitch so that you do not have to die this night," they said. "Take this knife, and plunge it into the heart of the prince. His blood will turn your feet back into a fish tail, and you will be able to live three hundred years in the sea, with us. Hurry! There is a pink haze on the horizon. Soon the sun will rise and you will die."

Chapter Eight

THE little mermaid pulled aside the cloth of the tent where the prince was sleeping. She crept inside and saw the bride sleeping peacefully with her head on the prince's chest. The little mermaid kissed the prince's forehead. He moved a little in his sleep and said his new wife's name. She alone was in his thoughts and dreams.

The sky was turning bright. The little mermaid's hand trembled around the knife. She could not kill her prince. She loosened her grip and threw the weapon into the sea. The waves turned red where it entered the water. The little mermaid looked once more at the prince before she threw herself into the sea after the knife.

She felt her body turning to foam. She felt the soft warmth of the sun. But the little mermaid did not feel death. Hundreds of ghostly forms floated above her. She could see through them to the clouds above. They spoke to her in voices so tender no humans could hear them.

When she looked down, the little mermaid saw that she was just like them.

"Who are you?" she asked, and her voice sounded as lovely as theirs.

"We are the daughters of the air," they told her. "Like mermaids, we do not have immortal souls. But we are allowed to win a soul by good deeds. We blow cooling winds to heal the sick. We take care of those on Earth. If we try to do what is good, we can win an immortal soul and live forever in happiness.

"You, little mermaid, have tried with all

of your heart to do what is good. That is why you are here with us. If you do good deeds, in three hundred years you, too, will win an immortal soul."

The little mermaid lifted her arms toward the sun and, for the first time, felt a tear on her cheek.

Below her on the ship the prince and princess had woken and were looking for her. They looked sadly into the sea as if they knew she had thrown herself into the waves. Though they could not see her, the little mermaid kissed the bride's forehead and smiled at the prince. Then she rose with the other children of the air into a passing pink cloud.

The Steadfast Tin Soldier

ONCE, long ago, there were twenty-five tin soldiers. They were all brothers, made from the same tin spoon, and lined up together in a box. When they were unpacked and allowed to see the light of day, "Tin soldiers!" were the first words they heard.

These words were shouted by the little boy who opened their box. He clapped his hands, for he was thrilled with his new toys. The boy put aside his other presents and lined the soldiers up on the table.

Standing at attention, the soldiers looked very smart. Each one carried his rifle on his shoulder and looked straight ahead. Each wore the same brightly painted red-and-blue uniform. They all looked exactly alike — except for one, the one who had been made last. There had not been enough tin to make the last soldier, so he had only one leg.

Nevertheless, this soldier stood as firmly on his one leg as the other soldiers did on two. And he was the only soldier who became a real hero.

On the table surrounding the soldiers were a great many toys. The most amazing toy was a pretty paper castle. Through the castle windows you could see many lovely rooms. The castle was surrounded by little trees. In front of it was a clear lake with wax swans swimming on it and admiring their own reflections, for the lake was really a mirror.

All of this was very pretty. But even prettier was the little dancer who stood in the castle's open door. She was cut out of paper and had a dress of white lace. Around her shoulders the dancer wore a thin blue ribbon like a scarf. On that ribbon was fixed a glittering tinsel rose as big as her face.

The little doll stood with both of her hands outstretched and one leg lifted high, so high that the tin soldier could not see it. He thought she had just one leg, like himself.

Why, she would be the perfect wife for me, the tin soldier thought. But he was worried. For the little doll was grand. She lived in a castle, while the soldier lived in a box that he shared with his twenty-four brothers.

I could never ask her to share a box with all of my brothers, he thought. Still, he longed to meet her. So he hid himself behind a snuffbox on the table. From there he had a perfect view of the tiny dancer who stood on one leg without ever losing her balance.

That night all of the other soldiers were put into their box. The people of the house went to bed. It was the time that the toys liked best — the time when they could play. They threw parties, fought battles, and danced until dawn.

What a racket they made! The chalk amused itself on the slate. The canary sang rhymes. The nutcrackers turned somersaults. And the poor tin soldiers rattled in their box. They wanted to play, too. But they could not lift the lid.

The tin soldier and the dancer were the only ones who stayed still. She stood on tiptoe, stretching out her arms. He stood still on his one leg, never taking his eyes off her.

When the clock struck twelve, the lid of the snuffbox that the tin soldier stood behind flew open, for it was not a snuffbox at all. It was a terrible jack-in-the-box. An ugly goblin head popped out.

"Keep your eyes to yourself," the goblin barked at the tin soldier.

The tin soldier was startled, but he pretended not to hear the ugly fellow.

"Suit yourself," said the scowling goblin. "You'll be sorry tomorrow."

When morning came and the children got up, the boy played with the one-legged soldier on the windowsill.

Was it the curse of the goblin or just a strong gust of wind that caused what happened next? We will never know. But while the tin soldier sat on the sill, the windows flew open, and he was swept outside. He fell headfirst down three stories and landed in the mud between the cobblestones. His one leg stuck up in the air. His bayonet was jammed into the wet dirt.

Of course the boy came down to look for the soldier immediately. But though he was so close that he almost stepped on the tiny tin man, the little boy did not see him.

The soldier wished he could cry out, "Here I am!" But he didn't think he should shout while in uniform, so he said nothing. When it started to rain, the boy went back inside.

The rain began as a drizzle but soon became a downpour. When the rain was over, two street boys wandered by.

"Look, a tin soldier," one of them cried. "I think he'd make a fine sailor!"

The other boy was holding a boat made of newspaper. He was just about to float it down the gutter. He stood the tin soldier in the bow. Then the boat was off!

The waves in the gutter were large, and the tin soldier had to hold himself very still to keep from trembling. He'd never been sailing before. The boys ran along the gutter excitedly as the newspaper boat was tossed in the current.

Suddenly, the boat was swept into a long, covered drain. The soldier could not see what was happening. It was as dark in the drain as it was in his box when the lid was shut.

This is all the goblin's fault, the soldier thought. Now I don't know where I am or where I will end up. If only the dancer were with me. Then I wouldn't mind the darkness.

A large water rat that lived in the drain swam alongside the boat.

"Have you got a pass?" the rat asked the tin soldier. "You must give me your pass."

The tin soldier held his rifle more tightly and kept his mouth shut. The boat rushed on.

The rat followed behind, but he could not keep up. "Stop him!" the rat squeaked. "He does not have a pass!"

There was no one to hear the rat, and the current was getting stronger and stronger. The paper boat floated quickly toward a spot of daylight. The tin soldier was happy to see some light — until he heard the roar of rushing water.

At the end of the drain, water poured out into a large canal. It might not seem dangerous to a human, but for the tin soldier it was like a huge waterfall. He was too close to the edge to stop his fall, so the tin soldier held himself as stiffly as he could. He did not blink. He did not flinch. He was very brave as he plunged out of the drain.

The boat whirled around two or three times. It filled to the brim with water and began to sink. The tin soldier stood at attention as the water reached his neck and then his chin. When the water closed over his head, he thought only of the sweet little dancer whom he would never see again.

Suddenly, before he could settle into the muddy canal bottom with the bits of paper boat, the tin soldier was snapped up and swallowed by a big fish.

It was very dark inside the fish, much darker than in the drain, and there wasn't much room. The soldier lay very still while the fish swam around, thrashing this way and that. At last the fish stopped swimming.

The tin soldier must have fallen asleep. Before he knew what had happened, he saw a flash like lightning and lay in broad daylight. A voice above him shouted, "The tin soldier!"

It was almost as exciting as when the soldier had first been unwrapped with his brothers. The fish that had swallowed him had been caught and taken to market. It was sold and brought to the kitchen of the very same house where the little boy lived. Then the fish was opened by the cook with a big knife.

The cook picked up the soldier, rinsed him off, and carried him upstairs to tell everyone about the little tin man's amazing travels.

The soldier was shocked to find himself standing on the very same table he had been on that morning. He looked around and saw the boy and the toys and the castle and, of course, the pretty dancer. She stood in the same spot with one leg held high in the air. She was steadfast.

The tin soldier would have shed tin tears had he not been in uniform. Instead he looked at the dancer and she looked back at him. Neither moved or said a word.

Then, without warning, the little boy's brother seized the tin soldier and threw him into the fireplace! There was no explanation, and we can only imagine that the jack-in-the-box goblin made him do it.

The tin soldier stood in the flames, staring out. The heat was almost unbearable, and he did not know if it was from the fire or from true love. His uniform was faded. Whether it was from his journey or from sorrow, we will never know.

He looked at the dancer and she looked back at him. He felt as if he were melting, but still he stood upright. He was steadfast.

All at once the window banged open and a gust of wind carried the dancer like a leaf into the flames — right next to the tin soldier. She burned brightly for a moment and was gone. The tin soldier melted slowly into a small lump.

The ashes were cleaned out the next morning. All that was left of the dancer was the tinsel rose, burned as black as coal. The soldier had melted and reformed into the shape of a little tin heart.

The Tinderbox

LEFT. Right. Left. Right. A soldier marched home along the road to his town. The war was over, but the soldier liked to march. Left. Right.

Halt. The soldier was most of the way home when he was stopped by a gruesome witch. Her face was gnarled, her hair was matted, and her bottom lip hung down almost to her waist.

"Good evening, soldier," she drooled. "What a fine sword you have, and what a large pack! You look like a true soldier, marching home after a job well done. And you shall be rewarded."

"Thank you, old witch," the soldier said.

He had never met a witch before and wasn't sure what to expect.

"Do you see that big tree?" the witch asked. She pointed to a tree just off the road. "It is hollow inside. Climb to the top of the tree and find the hole. Then lower yourself inside. I will tie this rope to your waist. When you call to me, I will pull you up."

"Why would I want to climb inside of that tree?" the soldier asked. He had heard that witches were not to be trusted.

"To get money!" the witch spat. "When you come to the bottom of the hole in the tree, you will be inside a great hall. Hundreds of lamps burn there, day and night.

"You will see three doors. Inside the first door is a large chest. On top of the chest is a dog with eyes as big as teacups. Never mind him. I will give you my apron to spread upon the floor. If you place the dog on the apron, he will do you no harm. Then you can open the chest. It is filled with copper coins. Take as many as you like.

"If you would rather have silver coins, go to the second room. There is another chest. Sitting on this one is a dog with eyes as big as wheels. Do not be afraid. Just put him on my apron and take as much money as you can carry.

"But perhaps you would prefer gold. In that case you should go to the third room. The dog there has eyes as big around as a tower. He is a fierce dog, I can tell you. But do not fear him. He will not hurt you if you place him on my apron. Then you can take as much gold from the chest as you please."

"That doesn't sound too bad," the soldier said. "But what do you want in return? I am sure you must want something."

"You are a good soldier, and clever," said the witch. "I will not ask you for a single coin. I only ask that you bring me an old tinderbox. My grandmother forgot it the last time she was in the tree."

The soldier agreed and let the witch tie the rope around his waist. Tucking the witch's apron into his belt, he climbed the tree and lowered himself into it. He found himself in a large chamber. It was just as the witch said it would be. There were hundreds of lamps and three big doors.

The soldier opened the first door and took a step back. A dog with eyes as big as teacups sat staring at him.

"You're a fine dog," the soldier said. He spread out the witch's apron and carefully lifted the dog onto it. The dog turned around once and lay down with its head on its paws.

The soldier opened the chest. It was filled with copper coins. He took as many as his pockets would hold, closed the chest, and put the dog back on top of it.

Next he went to the second room. Sitting on a chest was a dog with eyes as big as wheels.

"You ought not stare," the soldier told the dog. "You might strain your eyes." Then he placed the dog on the apron and opened the second chest. When he saw the silver coins, he emptied his pockets and filled them with silver instead. Then he filled his pack.

After placing the second dog back on the silver chest, the soldier entered the third room.

"Good evening," he said, tipping his hat. He was not sure what to do in front of a dog like this. When he could finally tear his gaze from the dog's tower-sized eyes, he placed him gently on the apron.

What a lot of gold there was in the third chest! The soldier did not waste a moment. He emptied his pockets and pack of silver and refilled them with gold. Then he filled his boots and hat with coins as well. When he was finished he could barely move!

He managed to get the dog back on the chest and closed the door. Then he called to the witch, "Pull me up!"

"Have you found my tinderbox?" she asked.

The soldier had forgotten all about the box. He rushed back to look for it. When he found it and had it safely tucked into his shirt, he called the old witch again, and she pulled him up.

Outside the tree, feeling very rich indeed, the soldier grew bold. "What will you do with the tinderbox?" he asked the ugly witch.

"That's none of your business," she hissed. "You have your money, now give me what's mine."

"Don't be rude," the soldier said. "Tell me what you're going to do with it or I'll draw my sword."

"Never," said the witch. She wiped some spittle from her chin.

The soldier had had enough of the old witch. He drew his sword and cut off her head. Then he tied up his gold in her apron, placed the tinderbox on top, and continued on his way.

When the soldier reached the town, he stayed at the best inn and asked for the best room. He ate his favorite meal for dinner. The next day he bought himself new boots and fine clothes.

Now that he was rich, the soldier looked like a real gentleman. And the people treated him like one. They told him all about the wonderful things in town. They talked about their gracious king and his daughter, the beautiful princess.

"How can I see her?" the soldier asked.

"You cannot," they all said. "She lives in a locked copper castle surrounded by high walls. Only the king holds the key. He is afraid that the princess will marry a simple soldier. It has been foretold, but the king will not allow it."

The soldier wanted to see the fair princess. But since there was little chance of getting permission from the king, he went on with his merry life.

The soldier went to the theater and drove around in a fancy carriage. He gave generously to the poor, for he remembered from his soldier days what it was like to be penniless. He had many friends who told him what a fine man he was.

Days passed, and the soldier kept spending money without earning any more. Soon he found himself with nothing but a single coin. He had to give up the elegant rooms he had lived in and move to the attic. None of his friends came to visit.

"There are too many stairs to climb," they said, and the soldier believed them.

One dark, cold evening the soldier was trying to mend his clothes. His candle sputtered to the end, and he hadn't the money to buy another. That's when he remembered that he had seen the stump of a candle in the witch's tinderbox.

The soldier had not thought about the tinderbox for a long time. But now he dug it from the bottom of his soldier's pack. He struck the flint once, to light the candle, and the door to the attic burst open. There sat the dog with eyes as large as teacups.

"What are your commands, my lord?" the dog asked.

"What's this!" the soldier exclaimed. He was more than a little bit surprised. He looked at the dented box in his hand. "This is a fine tinderbox indeed if it will get me whatever I wish for!"

The dog stood staring and waiting.

"Get me some money," the soldier said. In a flash the dog was gone and then back again with a sack of copper coins in its mouth.

The soldier quickly discovered that if he struck the box once, the dog from the first room appeared. If he struck twice, the second dog, which guarded the silver, arrived. And if he struck three times, the dog that guarded the gold came to do his bidding.

Soon he was back in his old rooms, wearing fine clothes and surrounded by friends. He began to think once more about the beautiful princess.

What good is her beauty if she has to stay locked up in a castle? he thought one night. Can I never get a look at her?

The soldier struck his tinderbox once, and the teacup-eyed dog instantly appeared.

"I know it's midnight," the soldier said to the dog, "but I would like to see the princess for just a moment."

The dog dashed out the door and was back in a flash. There, fast asleep on his back, was the princess. She was as lovely as everyone said. The soldier kissed her once and asked the dog to return her to her copper castle.

The next morning the princess told the king and queen about the strange dream she'd had about a dog and a soldier.

"What a pretty tale," the queen said. But that night the king had one of the court ladies sit by the princess's bed to make sure the dream was just that — a dream.

The soldier desperately wanted to see the princess again. So he sent one of the dogs again that night.

The dog picked up the princess and ran off with her as fast as he could. But the court lady pulled on her boots and followed, running as fast as the dog. She saw the door that the dog had disappeared into with the princess. Taking a piece of chalk, she marked it with a cross so that she would recognize the place in the morning. Then she went home to bed.

After only a moment the dog left again to take the princess back to the castle. On his way he noticed the mark the court lady had made. Picking up the chalk that the lady had dropped, the dog made crosses on every door in town.

The next morning the king, the queen, the lady, and the court officers strode into town to see where the princess had been taken by the dog.

"There it is," said the king. He pointed to a door with a white cross on it.

"No. Here it is, dear husband," said the queen. She was standing beside another door with a white mark.

"But there is another — and another," the officers cried.

It was pointless to try to locate the house where the princess had gone. The search was called off.

But the queen was a clever woman, and she did not give up. She stitched a small silk purse and filled it with buckwheat.

Then she cut a small hole in the corner and tied it to the princess's skirts. Now the princess could be tracked by a trail of buckwheat.

That night the dog came again, for the soldier had fallen in love with the princess. He wished more than anything that he were a prince so he could marry her.

The dog did not notice the buckwheat that fell along the road from the castle window to the soldier's house. But the king and queen saw it well enough the next day.

Very quickly the soldier was arrested and thrown into prison. It was dark and damp in the soldier's cell.

"Tomorrow you will be hanged," the jailer told him. The soldier knew he was doomed, for he did not have his tinderbox.

In the morning the soldier watched through the barred window as the townspeople hurried off to the place where he would be killed. The cobbler's boy was in such a rush to get there that one of his leather shoes slipped off. It landed against the wall next to the soldier.

"Don't be in such a hurry," the soldier said to the boy. "Nothing will happen before I get there. If you will run to my rooms and fetch my tinderbox, I will give you a copper coin!"

The cobbler's boy was eager to have a copper coin of his own, and the soldier's rooms were nearby. In only a moment the boy had his money and the soldier his box.

Outside town a large crowd stood around the gallows where the soldier was to be hanged. The king and queen sat on thrones, surrounded by the judges and council.

The soldier was taken to the gallows and soon stood at the top of a ladder. He was not scared. Just before the rope was put around his neck the soldier spoke.

"It is customary to grant a last request

to a poor criminal," he said loudly. "And I would like, for my last act in this world, to smoke a pipe."

The king could not deny so small a request in front of such a crowd. So the soldier pulled his tinderbox from his pocket. One. One, two. One, two, three times the soldier struck the box. One, two, three dogs appeared.

"Help me," the soldier commanded them. "Save me from being hanged."

The dogs charged toward the judges and council. They grabbed them by the legs and tossed them so far into the air that they never came back. Then the dogs seized the king and queen and threw them after the others.

The people in the crowd saw how powerful the soldier was with the help of his dogs. And they remembered his kindness before he had been put in jail.

"You shall be our king," they cried. "You shall marry the princess."

It was more than the soldier had hoped. The crowd lifted him up and carried him to the king's waiting carriage. The dogs ran ahead, and the people cheered as the soldier rode off to free the beautiful princess.

The wedding festivities were grand indeed. They lasted eight days. Everyone was overjoyed. The soldier finally had his princess. The princess loved the soldier almost as much as she loved being queen. And the dogs wagged their tails as they sat at the banquet table staring at everyone through their giant eyes.

Thumbelina

Chapter One

ONCE there was a woman who wanted a child more than anything. But she did not know where to find one. Feeling very lonely, she went to a witch and told her of her longing.

"A small child?" the witch replied. "Why, that's as easy as winking! Take this barley seed. It is not the kind of barley that grows in the fields or is fed to chickens. No. Put this seed in a flowerpot and tend it carefully. Then you shall see what sort of seed it is."

The woman thanked the witch and gave her a few coins. Then she rushed home and planted the tiny seed, just as the witch had told her to do.

No sooner had she gotten the seed in the soil than a flower sprang up. It looked just like a large tulip with a tightly closed bud.

"What a lovely flower!" the woman exclaimed. She bent to kiss the yellow-and-red petals. The moment the woman's lips touched the flower, it burst open. It was a real tulip. And sitting inside was a girl. The girl was perfect in every way, lovely and graceful and very, very tiny. When the woman picked her up, she saw that the girl was scarcely as big as her thumb! She named her Thumbelina.

The woman loved Thumbelina from the start and cared for her well. At night Thumbelina slept in a polished walnut-shell cradle with a violet-petal mattress and a rose-petal quilt. During the day she played on the table. She sailed across a plate of water ringed with flowers on a red tulip petal. Two white horsehairs were her oars. And she sang in a delicate, silvery voice like none other.

Chapter Two

ONE night as Thumbelina lay sleeping in her cozy bed, a toad hopped in the window. It was a big toad, wet and very ugly. It hopped right down to where Thumbelina lay sleeping under her red-rose blanket.

"What a lovely wife for my son!" the toad said. Without even looking around, the toad picked up the walnut shell and hopped off with it into the garden.

She took Thumbelina to the muddy edge of a broad stream. There she lived with her son, who was as horrible and ugly as his mother.

"Look what I have brought you," said

the mother toad proudly. She showed Thumbelina to her son.

"Koaks, koaks, brekke-ke-kex," was all he could say.

"Don't talk so loud, or you'll wake her," the old toad scolded. "And she might flee, for she is as light as swansdown. We will put her on a water lily leaf. She is so small it will be like an island for her. Then she cannot escape while we prepare a home for the two of you under the mud."

In the middle of the stream a mass of water lilies grew. Their broad green leaves floated on the water. The old toad swam to the largest one — the one that was farthest out — and put Thumbelina in her walnut shell upon it.

When Thumbelina awoke in the morning and looked around, she started to cry. She was surrounded by water and could not get back to shore.

The old toad was busy decorating her

son's new home with rushes and water-weeds. When she was ready to furnish it, she swam out to the lily leaf with her son to fetch Thumbelina's bed.

The old toad bowed before Thumbelina. "Let me introduce my son," she croaked. "He will soon be your husband. You will share a lovely home in the mud."

"Koaks, koaks, brekke-ke-kex," was all the son could say.

As the toads swam away with her bed, Thumbelina cried even harder. She did not want to live in the mud or marry a toad!

The fish swimming nearby had heard what the old toad said. They felt sorry for Thumbelina. So they crowded around the stem that held the lily leaf in place and nibbled away. Before long the leaf was floating down the stream, taking Thumbelina far, far away.

Chapter Three

THE leaf sailed gently down the stream. Thumbelina passed through towns and forests. Soon she stopped crying. She was far from the toad, and there were many pretty things to see.

Birds in the bushes saw her and sang out, "What a lovely little girl!"

A delicate white butterfly flew around and around Thumbelina. At last it landed on her leaf. Thumbelina gently tied one end of her sash to the butterfly and fastened the other end to the leaf. The butterfly flew along, pulling the leaf like a boat. Now Thumbelina traveled much faster than before.

Suddenly, a large beetle flew by and

grabbed Thumbelina around the middle. He flew up into a tree with Thumbelina tight in his claws. The lily leaf went floating on, taking the butterfly with it.

Thumbelina was very frightened. But more than that she was worried about the butterfly. She hoped that he could get free and would not starve to death, attached to the lily.

The beetle did not care one bit. He sat beside Thumbelina on the biggest leaf in the tree. He told Thumbelina she was very pretty — though she did not look at all like a beetle — and handed her the sweetest parts of the flowers to eat.

A little while later all of the other beetles in the tree came by to visit. When they saw Thumbelina, they turned up their feelers.

"Look at her legs!" they cried. "She only has two! And her waist is so narrow. She hasn't got any feelers. Why, she looks just like a human! It's disgusting. Disgraceful."

Each of the beetles declared they had never seen anything as ugly as Thumbelina.

Of course, Thumbelina wasn't ugly. And the beetle that carried her off thought she was very pretty. But when all of his friends said that she was ugly he changed his mind and decided he didn't want to keep her any longer. He flew with her to the base of the tree and dropped her in a daisy.

Chapter Four

ALL summer long Thumbelina lived by herself in the great wood. She wove a bed of grass stems and hung it like a hammock under a wild rhubarb, which protected her from the rain. She drank nectar from flowers and sipped dew from the leaves every morning. In the evening she rocked in her hammock and listened to the birds. Thumbelina was very happy.

But summer ended and fall arrived. The birds that sang so sweetly all flew away. The flowers faded and died, and the rhubarb leaf she used for shelter shriveled into a dry yellow stalk.

After the fall came the long, bleak winter. Thumbelina was dreadfully cold. Her clothes were in rags, and she was so small! It began to snow, and every snowflake was to her like a whole shovelful of snow is to a human. She wrapped herself up in a withered leaf, but still she shivered.

Thumbelina had to do something. So she walked and walked through the woods until she came to the edge of a cornfield. The corn had gone to seed. All that was left were dry stalks sticking up from the frozen ground.

At last Thumbelina came to a hole — the door to a field mouse house. Inside it was snug and warm. She passed a room full of corn, a cozy kitchen, and even a pantry.

Thumbelina was hoping the field mouse would give her a bit of barleycorn. She hadn't eaten in days. When the field mouse saw Thumbelina, looking just like a beggar girl, she felt sorry for her.

"You poor thing," the mouse said. "You had better come into my warm room and have dinner with me."

It was not long before the field mouse had invited Thumbelina to stay through the winter. Not only was she a kind-hearted creature, she liked Thumbelina very much.

"But you must keep the rooms neat and tell me stories, for I am very fond of them," the field mouse said.

Thumbelina was happy to do what was asked, and she led a very nice life with the good-hearted field mouse.

One day the field mouse told Thumbelina that she must tidy up with extra care. "My neighbor comes to visit once a week," she explained. "He is even better off than I am. He lives in several large rooms and wears the most beautiful black velvet coat. If he were to marry you, you would live very well! But he is blind. Since he cannot see you, you must tell him pretty stories to earn his favor."

Thumbelina did as she was asked. But she did not want to marry the neighbor. He was, after all, a mole.

Thumbelina told the mole all about the flowers that grew aboveground in the summer. But he did not like the sun, and so he did not like these stories.

She sang to him about ladybugs and mulberry bushes. The mole did not like the words, but he soon fell in love with Thumbelina's voice. On his next visit he invited Thumbelina and the field mouse to see his fine house.

Chapter Five

THE mole had recently finished digging a passage between his house and the mouse's. Lighting the way with a bit of torchwood, he led them through the dim, twisting passage. After several turns they came upon a swallow lying in the path. It looked as if it were dead. Its eyes were closed, and its pretty wings were folded tightly to its sides. It had, no doubt, been killed by the cold.

Thumbelina felt sorry for the little fellow. She was fond of birds, for they had sung to her and kept her company all through the summer. But the mole kicked at the swallow with his stumpy legs.

"He won't be making a racket any-more," the mole said. "How awful it must be to be born a bird. A bird does nothing but sing and fly about. It hasn't even the sense not to starve in winter."

"What's the use of a birdsong?" the field mouse agreed. "A song cannot keep you alive in the cold."

Thumbelina said nothing. When the others had continued on their way, she bent and kissed the little bird. "You might have been one that sang so prettily to me this summer," she whispered.

Later that night Thumbelina could not sleep. She got up and wove a blanket out of hay. Then she crept down the passage and tucked the blanket around the little bird.

"Good-bye, swallow," she said. "Thank you for your song this summer, when the trees were green and the sun warmed us so nicely."

Thumbelina lay her head on the bird's soft breast — and jumped back in fright. Something was stirring inside the bird!

It was the swallow's steady heartbeat. The little bird was not dead after all. He'd just been numb with cold. Thumbelina's warmth and blanket had brought him back to life!

Every night Thumbelina snuck back to visit the little bird. When he was strong enough to speak, he thanked Thumbelina. "At last my strength is returning. Soon I shall fly again in the warm sunshine," he sang.

"Not yet," Thumbelina said. "You must rest in your bed. Outside it is still snowy and cold."

The swallow told her how he had torn one of his wings on a thorn. When the other birds flew away to warmer places, he could not keep up. He had fallen and could not remember anything more.

Thumbelina brought the bird food and

water all winter long. But she never told the mouse or the mole, since they did not like birds.

When spring came, it was time for the bird to say good-bye. He poked a hole in the ground over his bed and the sun shone through it.

"Come with me," the swallow begged Thumbelina. "You can sit on my back and we'll fly into the woods."

"I can't," Thumbelina replied. She was very sad to see the swallow go, but she could not leave the field mouse. The swallow thanked Thumbelina again. Then he flew away into the sunny sky.

Chapter Six

POOR Thumbelina was not allowed to go out in the sunshine. The field mouse made her work every day on her wedding clothes. Every evening the mole came and asked her to sing until she was hoarse.

It had been decided that Thumbelina and the mole should be married in the fall. But Thumbelina still did not want to marry the mole. She felt as if all of her happiness had flown off with the swallow. But the field mouse told her to be grateful. For the mole loved her and would take good care of her.

The days grew shorter, and each evening Thumbelina snuck out of the mouse hole. She could not stay out long.

But she knew that these were the last days she would ever see the sun. Once she was married she would live with the mole under the ground forever.

The evening before the wedding, Thumbelina came out of the hole to say a final farewell to the outside world. She was so sad that she began to cry.

"Good-bye, bright sun," she wept. "Good-bye, flowers." She threw her arms around a tiny red bloom that had not yet faded away. "Give the swallow my love if you see him." Thumbelina buried her head in a leaf.

Suddenly, she heard a birdsong. It was the swallow flying overhead! He had come looking for Thumbelina.

"The cold winter is coming," the swallow said. "Won't you come with me now? I am flying to warmer places where it is always summer and there are always lovely flowers."

"I will come with you," Thumbelina

said. She felt badly about leaving the field mouse, but she could not bring herself to marry the mole. So she climbed on the bird's back and placed her feet on his outstretched wings.

Up they flew, into the air. They soared over forests and lakes and snow-covered mountains. Thumbelina lay snugly under the swallow's feathers, looking at the beauty beneath her.

Chapter Seven

AT last Thumbelina and the swallow arrived in a warmer country. The land was even more wonderful than Thumbelina had imagined. Lemons and oranges hung from the trees. There were flowers everywhere. The sun shone brighter than on the brightest summer day.

The little bird took Thumbelina to the home of the swallows. "This is my house," he said. "Now you must choose one for yourself." The swallow flew over the flowers that grew below his nest. "Choose any flower," he told her, "and we shall be neighbors."

Thumbelina pointed to a large white blossom. The swallow swooped down and placed her on one of the petals. She slipped inside.

But there was already someone inside the flower!

A little man, the same size as Thumbelina, sat in the middle of the flower. He had delicate wings and a tiny gold crown. The flowers around them held many more men and women. The little man in Thumbelina's flower was their king.

"Isn't he wonderful?" Thumbelina whispered to the swallow. Never before had she seen anyone her size.

And never before had the little king seen anyone as beautiful as Thumbelina. He took the crown from his head and put it gently onto hers. Then he asked her to be his queen — and queen of all the flowers.

"Yes," Thumbelina answered happily. At last she felt as if she had found a perfect home.

Men and women began to emerge from

other flowers. They all wanted to meet their new queen. They even gave Thumbelina her own pair of wings so she could fly from flower to flower.

Thumbelina had never been so happy. Everyone celebrated all day and well into the night. And above them the swallow sang his very best song.